How
Do You
Dance?

Like this!

Thyra Heder

Abrams Books for Young Readers • New York

Like this!

Like this!

Like this!

I don't...

I do!

Rick does, too!

GO RICK!

Mags beckons.

Koyo bops.

Gilda flits.

Aurora scrunches.

C.J. makes a face
like something stinks.

John looks
right at you.

Just move a part, then move another.
Let it get weird.
See where it goes!

FACE

FINGERS

KNEES

TOES

Maybe
you
have
no
bones.

Maybe
you
are
made
of metal.

Maybe you shimmy because you
made something delicious.

Like so, so, SO DELISH—

Yum
yum
Yum.

HEY!!

MAYBE
You don't want
to dance
and just want
to eat dinner.
OKAY?!

Okay.
No dancing during dinner.

But you *could* dance . . .

After dinner!

At the market!

At the bus stop!

On a break!

Good days!

Rainy days.

Sad days, even.

Sometimes you just need to flop around . . .

. . . until you feel better.

TRY SOME

THE JIGGLE

THE SWIVEL

THE FLAP

THE ZAPPO

THE ZIP

THE MISTER

THE SNEAK

THE WINDY

THE TOODLE

NEW MOVES!

THE SLIP

THE SCRIBBLE

THE MIDDLE

THE SISTER

THE POODLE

THE SCOOT

THE NOTHING

Oh!

How do you do
The Nothing?

You just do NOTHING.

Fine.

THE POOT

Go HIGH!

Down
LOW.

FAST FAST

FAST!

Then slooooooowwwww.

Dinos!

Robos!

Horsies!

Dads!

ALL TOGETHER

IN THE DARK!

ENOUGH!!

I don't dance like that.

I want to be left alone.

Understood.
But just between us . . .

How *do* you dance?

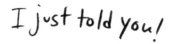

Alone!

For everyone dancing everywhere
—T. H.

The illustrations in this book were made with pencil and watercolor
and by watching and making a lot of dance videos.

ISBN 978-1-4197-3418-2

Library of Congress Control Number 2018966486

Text and illustrations copyright © 2019 Thyra Heder
Book design by Pamela Notarantonio

Printed and bound in U.S.A.
10 9 8 7 6 5 4 3 2

Abrams Books for Young Readers are available at special
discounts when purchased in quantity for premiums and promotions
as well as fundraising or educational use. Special editions
can also be created to specification. For details, contact
specialsales@abramsbooks.com or the address below.

ABRAMS The Art of Books
195 Broadway, New York, NY 10007
abramsbooks.com